W9-ABO-823

Artforum

Markham Public Library
Thornhill Village Branch
10 Colborne Street
Thornhill, ON L3T 1Z6
Aug 2020

ALSO BY CÉSAR AIRA FROM NEW DIRECTIONS

Birthday

Conversations

Dinner

Ema, the Captive

An Episode in the Life of a Landscape Painter

Ghosts

The Hare

How I Became a Nun

The Linden Tree

The Literary Conference

The Little Buddhist Monk and *The Proof*

The Miracle Cures of Dr. Aira

The Musical Brain

The Seamstress and the Wind

Shantytown

Varamo

Artforum

•

CÉSAR AIRA

Translated by Katherine Silver

A NEW DIRECTIONS PAPERBOOK ORIGINAL

Copyright © 2014 by César Aira
Translation copyright © 2020 by Katherine Silver

Originally published by Blatt & Ríos, Buenos Aires, in 2014; published
in conjunction with the Literary Agency Michael Gaeb/Berlin

All rights reserved. Except for brief passages quoted in a newspaper,
magazine, radio, television, or website review, no part of this book may
be reproduced in any form or by any means, electronic or mechanical,
including photocopying and recording, or by any information storage
and retrieval system, without permission in writing from the Publisher.

Manufactured in the United States of America
First published as a New Directions Paperbook (NDP1472) in 2020
New Directions books are published on acid-free paper
Design by Erik Rieselbach

Library of Congress Cataloging-in-Publication Data
Names: Aira, César, 1949– author. | Silver, Katherine, translator.
Title: Artforum / César Aira ; translated by Katherine Silver.
Other titles: Artforum. English
Description: New York : New Directions Publishing Corporation, 2020. |
Identifiers: LCCN 2019043237 | ISBN 9780811229265 (paperback ; acid-free
paper) | ISBN 9780811229272 (ebook)
Classification: LCC PQ7798.1.I7 A8313 2020 | DDC 863/.64—dc23
LC record available at https://lccn.loc.gov/2019043237

10 9 8 7 6 5 4 3 2 1

New Directions Books are published for James Laughlin
by New Directions Publishing Corporation
80 Eighth Avenue, New York 10011

Some say that I am a genius, others that I am a mad-man. I'm neither one nor the other. The problem is, I read foreign magazines.

—A Chilean politician

ARTFORUM

The Sacrifice

I WOKE UP LATE, BLESSED BY THE SOUND OF rain, so merciful this oppressive summer; I had slept well thanks to the drop in temperature, and I almost could have kept sleeping ... I looked at my wristwatch, which I always left on the corner of my bedside table when I went to sleep, and it was eight o'clock, one hour later than I usually get up. I stretched voluptuously, Liliana mumbled something without waking up. The whispering of the rain was constant; the tires of the cars driving along the blue-gray paving stones on Calle Bonifacio produced that damp clicking sound that we city dwellers learn to recognize. It was Saturday, there were no commitments or schedules or predicaments. The kids were asleep.

Nevertheless, a faint alarm bell was going off in one corner of my brain, so faint that it took a while to become conscious, and even then it didn't worry

3

me very much; it didn't even make me speed up the
process of rising from bed, which I carried out at my
usual calm pace, moving in slow motion with long
pauses between one movement and the next in the
bedroom's greenish half-light. That modest alarm
was the same one I always felt when it rained in the
summer: it had become a conditioned reflex. The
thing is, because of the heat, we left all the windows
open night and day, and near the windows there
were tables, chairs, and armchairs, and on these
were books and magazines; there was an enormous
amount of paper in the house. All of us in the family were readers, the bookshelves were overflowing,
books and magazines were piled everywhere. It was
inevitable that some would be within reach of the
rain, which could come in through the open windows. It's well known how destructive water is to paper. Once, many years before, I had had an unfortu-
nate experience in that respect. I was alone at home
on a suffocatingly hot day. I went out, and during
my absence it started to rain, a violent downpour
that forced me to wait for a while in a café; when I
returned I found that water had entered through a
window, and a beautiful little illustrated book about

insects, which I greatly valued, had gotten wet, and it was definitively damaged, even though I made every effort to dry it; it remained crumpled and wavy, and I reproached myself bitterly. I'm not a bibliophile collector and I mostly keep my perfectionism in check, but I take good care of books.

The truth is, that accident long ago was the only one I had to regret, but it was enough to instill me with prudence, which like everything in me, took on a tinge of fanaticism over time. Or confirmed it, because the fanaticism was already there. As soon as the first drop of rain fell, I'd run through the apartment, window by window, almost always without closing them because it could rain without water entering; this depended on the rain, and since our apartment was on a corner, whatever was happening at the windows that opened onto one street did not necessarily indicate what was happening at those that opened onto the other. Whenever I was going out and a storm was threatening, I'd ask Liliana if she was staying home, and if she said yes, I'd tell her to close the windows if it started to rain, or to keep an eye on them; if she had plans to go out, I'd take the precaution of closing them before I left.

My main concern was the living room window that opened onto Calle Bonorino; that window was behind my favorite armchair, next to which, just under the window, was a glass table where I always kept, right at hand, the magazines I was currently reading.

So many years had passed without any losses that on that morning I didn't rush to check anything, even though I knew we had gone to sleep with all the windows open. Summer rains, so welcome after a spell of hot weather, tend to be vertical, polite, inoffensive. The sound I had started hearing while asleep and when I woke up didn't raise any red flags. Moreover, there is a psychological mechanism that creates compensatory optimism whenever you spend too much time worrying about something happening, thereby expelling the feared event from reality. Nevertheless, I made my usual rounds before doing anything else.

Halfway through my circuit, my calm was suddenly shattered. Through one window I saw the foliage on the trees shaking violently. We lived on the second floor, at the height of the treetops, which on Calle Bonifacio were dense and touched one another. I was surprised to see them shaking so violently, because I hadn't heard any wind. I realized that I hadn't heard it till that moment because I hadn't thought about it. My attention had been focused on the murmurings of the rain, and I dismissed the muffled hissing that accompanied it. Suddenly I heard it, as if the radio had been switched to a different station. And I heard it retrospectively because I had been hearing it the whole time. The green mass of leaves was leaning toward my left, in the direction of Camacuá, and that, I noted below the threshold of thought, meant that the wind was blowing from the most dangerous angle, the one that affected the window behind my armchair. As happens at moments of greatest alarm, a thousand images raced through my mind, including an inventory of the magazines I had been reading those last few days and that were piled next to my armchair.

I ran into the living room. In a way, I had already foreseen the worst, but I never could have foreseen everything. This was because of simultaneity. My mind got ahead of my eyes, my eyes got ahead of my mind, the two waited for each other so that they would coincide, making time go backwards. But time had already passed, and what I feared most had happened. The window was open, water had entered. I ran to close it and a few drops wet my arms.

On top of the glass end table that had been exposed to the rain was a pile of magazines, three or four. In that simultaneity, I remembered that the week before I had bought several magazines and had been skipping around, reading one then the other, one article in one, another in another. They were one *Artforum*, two *Art in America*, and one *Burlington Magazine*. I was truly passionate about these art magazines, which made me dream, stimulated me, inspired me. They were not easy to procure in Buenos Aires. My very last purchase had included a lucky find after a long period of nothing, and it had been a blast of pure oxygen for my snobby lungs. My favorite was *Artforum*, to which I have been faithful for years, and recounting my adventures to acquire it would fill a book. It was my luxury, my fantasy. I was gripped by incommensurate anxiety when I lowered my eyes to assess the damage. I was sure, with that certainty about misfortune that rarely errs, that an *Artforum* had been on the top of the pile: unconsciously I always left one there, because the mere sight of its cover lifted my spirits.

To my great dismay, on top of the pile of magazines was a ball, a sphere the size of a soccer ball and brightly colored, whose layout I recognized without recognizing it. That ball had not existed in my house the day before. It was new. It could not have entered through the window, which had a screen. It had formed inside. This chain of reasoning paraded through my brain in a few tenths of a second, during which time I already knew what I was seeing; I'd known it from the start but refused to believe it. The ball was the *Artforum*, its surface was the cover, showing the work of Robert Mangold. The same subliminal sight that had given me comfort for a week every time I was in the living room did a cruel somersault in my perceptions.

I touched it. With extreme caution, I picked it up. It was cold and wet to the touch, very heavy. It wasn't dripping, despite being full of water. Though difficult for me to admit, the only explanation was that it had absorbed the rain until it had acquired that perfectly spherical shape. With reverential care, I placed it on the tea cart on the other side of the armchair. It was a marvelous object, almost supernatural. When I was finally able to tear my eyes away, I looked at the other magazines, and that's when the true surprise set in.

The others were dry, intact. Not a single drop had touched them. I confirmed this by picking them up and passing the palms of my hands over the covers and along the edges. I leaned over the glass of the table, and there wasn't a trace of water there, either. Everything that had come through the window, then, had been absorbed by the *Artforum*, which hadn't let the tiniest bit escape.

I sat down, overwhelmed by this evidence, and little by little tried to put my ideas in order. The first, as well as the last, was that the *Artforum* had sacrificed itself to save the other magazines, like a magical and heroic soldier stepping out in front of his platoon under a barrage of firepower and taking all the bullets in his body without letting a single one hit his companions. But was that possible? The merely physical solutions had to be rejected. The paper *Artforum* is printed on is glossy, the least ab- sorbent paper in the world. This didn't mean water wouldn't damage it, and the other magazines, also printed on that shiny paper, would also have been ruined. But how, then, had it managed to restruc- ture itself in order to be able to seize each and every drop of rain that entered the window? By making a decision, apparently. There was no need to turn to a category as grandiose as the supernatural. I had noticed that things sometimes acted in accordance with their own decisions, that they had whims, fantasies, cruelties, as well as tenderness and generosity. As for the perfectly round form it had taken, this could be explained by *Artforum*'s peculiar, almost square, format.

That this was the one that had sacrificed itself for the others must have been because it was on top of the pile. Any other in its position would have done the same thing. Or not? There was something very suggestive in the fact that the martyr was precisely my favorite magazine, the one that most inspired me, the one I spent the most effort finding and that was the most difficult to find. I would have sacrificed all the others for it, but it had sacrificed itself for the others, with that divine automatism things have.

I woke up from my reverie staring at the spherical *Artforum*, from which I had not moved my eyes. It was an inexpressibly beautiful object, even though I could no longer look through it or read it. Useless and unreadable, I loved it more than ever. I asked myself a strange question, justified only by the strangeness of the situation: did it love me? If the purpose of its sacrifice was to save the other magazines, and I was the owner and reader of those magazines, then it had placed more value on my happiness than on its own life, and objectively that seemed like love. (But how wrong it was! Because I loved it more than all the other magazines combined.)

Can an object love a man? The entire history of animism was contained in that question. But anthropologists who had tried to answer it had never had the opportunity, as I had, to pose it while face-to-face with an object that had offered the supreme proof of love. It was not as impossible as it seemed at first sight. Objects were carriers of information. All of them, from cathedrals to little balls of mercury, were inscribed with their histories, their properties, their user manuals. That they did this in a mute, sometimes enigmatic, language did not detract from their eloquence. You only had to decipher them. Objects called books (and more so, magazines) fulfilled their condition as objects twice over by being specialized carriers of information; they were superobjects, because in their infinite variety and novelty they could supplant all other objects in imagination and desire.

That said, the quantum of information carried by objects was measured by the void of knowledge in the subject that confronted them, in other words, by their capacity to fill a hole that was preexisting and previously inhabited by desire. Love was very similar. Within emptiness's attraction to fullness dwelled an inevitable delay, because there was always a new plenitude, absent and remote. Perhaps all nostalgia and longing are derived from this: the inability of signs to adjust to the present. The regularity of magazines was the scenario of this drama.

I speak from experience because none of this was new for me: it came from my childhood in Pringles. Those remote provincial towns were nothing if they weren't austere. They were contaminated by the plains, whose fertile soil produced wealth without objective and without objects. Maybe it's an illusion, the same one felt by all young people who need to fill up their lives. I felt it sharply on the intellectual level. Even though I had all the books I wanted, there was something else I could never hope to amass, because it was being produced in time: magazines, current magazines, illustrated magazines. In them I found an object that created a formidable absence, a void that I suffered and that enhanced my capacity to read the world. In that empty town, everything became remote, and as the years passed my longing to leave grew.

I remembered a conversation I had with my father, one afternoon when we were alone in the large showroom of his shop, looking out at the deserted streets of the town. I must have been eleven or twelve. It had started to rain. I don't know what he might have said, probably something about how timely the rain was. I wanted to make a defiant statement to assert my independence, and I said: "I couldn't care less if it rains or not. It doesn't matter to me." "Yes it does," he answered. "No. Not to me. Why should it matter to me?" "Because the harvest, whether it's good or bad, depends on the rain, and my store does only as well as the farmers do ..." My father sold parts for agricultural equipment, and he was involved in other ventures related to farming. "... And our economic situation will affect you." He meant that everything was connected, even I, the least connected person in the world. For me it was a revelation, and not so much because the idea seemed new but precisely because I had already thought it, more than once; hearing it proved that others could also think it, which proved that everything was connected.

Perhaps the effect of that revelation was also due to the part played by the rain. That faraway place

where the magazines came from, that faraway place
where the present existed, was subject to a thousand
chances. Rain was intractable, capricious, as real as
reality; in other words, like the wall that desires and
fantasies crashed up against. And it also came from
far away, carried by the wind, which blew wherever
it wanted. And when it rained, it became the present: everything was tied together in a great web of
interconnectedness.

JANUARY 8, 1983

The Beggar

I NEVER GIVE HANDOUTS BECAUSE I CON-
sider it to be a futile act, like other activities on the
street, for example, muggings: the mugger remains
poor, the muggee remains rich, and the mugger is
forced to periodically repeat his offense because
what he acquires through it—product not pro-
ducer—runs out. I wonder if it's the same with every social interaction. Probably not. In any case, I
think it unwise of me to generalize on this subject
because I could slip into nihilism.

Begging manifests its futility through the repetition which it comprises. It is overwhelmingly sterile.
The only thing that could save it from such empty
automatism, or at least give it some variety, would
be the invention of stories and costumes used to try
to swindle the credulous donor. But anything colorful these creations might offer is canceled out by the
mental attitude with which it is received, according

to the maxim *caritas omnia credit*, "charity believes everything," which places this theological virtue on the level of state-subsidized poetry: why make an effort if payment is guaranteed beforehand? Why invent an ingenious story to extract a coin from a stranger if the most hackneyed pitch will work just as well?

But once, extemporaneously, I broke my own rule, and I did so with the excess that is typical of the unrepeatable. I gave a beggar who was asking for "spare change" a ten peso bill, that is, ten dollars. It was a fleeting moment, I didn't stop to watch the effect it produced. There was nothing special about the beggar. To tell the truth, I barely looked at him. Nor did I think much about my motivation. Why did I do it? Just because. For no reason. A gratuitous act, paradoxically gratuitous for it was an exchange of money.

Though, given my habit of realistic fantasizing, I obviously asked myself what the man might have done with those ten pesos. Not much. They meant nothing to me: I had many ten pesos. But for him, who had only one, it could mean a meal, a couple of cartons of cheap wine, if that was his priority. You must reach extreme poverty and neglect to achieve a realistic idea of a monetary unit.

I thought about it while sitting in my armchair, leafing through an *Artforum*. My eyes alighted upon the upper left corner of the cover, right where the price was: ten dollars. A world of equivalences opened up before me. The figure, so small for me, had been important to the beggar. But for me, too, it was important, and it became important again at that moment, because it represented an *Artforum*, which to me was a treasure. There was a comedic symmetry. The amount of money that for the beggar meant appeasing his hunger, for me gratified an idle whim, the snobbism of an armchair connoisseur. The movement went in only one direction, but it did so with the gentle yet invincible strength of the tides. The human began to permeate the magazine I held in my hands.

The miracle of convertibility had placed in communication poverty and wealth, New York and Buenos Aires, the primitivism of hunger and thirst and the elaborate glamour of contemporary art. A "miserable miracle," as Michaux would call it. This convertibility, which has made *Artforum* so cheap for me, makes me uneasy. I don't know where the catch might be as far as macroeconomics goes, but I think it violates a principle of logic as elemental as identity. If A equals B, B equals A. One dollar is worth one peso, something that makes all of us very happy, but one peso is not worth one dollar, not by a long shot. Where are we going to find a North American willing to buy one of our poor pesos with one of their precious dollars?

JUNE 28, 1997

Subscription

WHEN I MADE THE TRANSCENDENT DECISION to take out a subscription, I thought that all my problems were over. It wasn't easy, I had to overcome the internal resistance of the primitive economist that I was, who didn't buy anything if I couldn't hold it in my hands and pay with banknotes I pulled out of my pocket. I had never taken out a subscription to any magazine, and it was strange that I hadn't subscribed to *Artforum* until then, not only because it was my favorite magazine but because of how difficult it had always been to procure it. One day I will tell the story of the strategies I used, the travelers who brought it to me, the excursions I took to places that had it, or didn't have it, the providers I placed my hopes in, and those who let me down. I never failed to follow up on a lead, no matter how dubious it was. This story would almost be an autobiography; years of plenty, years of want, that's

what my life consisted of. I talked about this with
everybody; I didn't hide my quest from anybody,
because there was always the latent possibility that
somebody would know something, would point
me in a promising direction. Everybody asked me
why I didn't subscribe. Wasn't that the most logical,
the most rational, step? That's what subscriptions
were for, and anyway they were especially common
in the United States, where the majority of magazines are distributed by mail to subscribers. Why
hadn't I done it? I could list a thousand reasons: I
didn't have a credit card, I didn't know how to send
money or buy a check in dollars, I didn't trust the
postal service ... They weren't serious reasons. To
process the payments I could ask advice from my
many friends with subscriptions to foreign magazines; and the truth is, I never distrusted the postal
service, on the contrary, I am one of the few people
who has never been afflicted with that fear. I think I
didn't subscribe because deep down I never consid-
ered it necessary. I could spend an entire year without finding a single *Artforum* in all of Buenos Aires,
but I knew that sooner or later I would find one,
and I knew and anticipated the pleasure I would de-

rive from such a discovery. Or perhaps I magically feared the interruption of the long series of discoveries and disappointments, of that rhythm without rhythm my life had come to terms with since my youth.

So, what made me decide? I don't know that, either. Just because, to try something new, because the circumstances were right. A bank unexpectedly gave me a credit card (without my asking for it), I had spent almost a year without finding a single *Artforum*, and I discovered that there was a very easy way to subscribe on the Internet ... Finally: I did it. Perhaps it had become too absurd not to. The following day they sent me an email saying that my subscription had been received and they were sending me *the last issue* (they wrote in English), and they even added warm regards: "*best wishes for you in Argentina.*" My poor country was on the front pages of newspapers all over the world because of certain economic catastrophes. It must have caught their attention that in the middle of the financial, social, and political disaster, an Argentinean would take the initiative to subscribe to a sophisticated art magazine. But my money was worth the same as anybody else's; indeed, I paid at the end of the month when the first credit card statement arrived, and by then I had already received the first issue, *the last issue*, which gave me great joy.

I read it, I reread it, I endlessly looked through the pages, from back to front, from front to back, I held on to it while I was watching television, I lent it to Ernesto, he gave it back, I went back to reading it. That was in July. The issue they sent me was their Summer issue, from June, and for the following two months, during the summer holidays, the magazine isn't published. I had to wait till September, which I did happily, optimistic and trusting, without any impatience. I felt this *Artforum* to be both more valuable and less valuable than the innumerable other ones that had come into my hands over the past twenty years. I hadn't found it, chance and luck had played no part, it was not a miracle; but it was the first one that had come directly to me from "the factory"; it was the dawn of a new era in my life, more automatic, more predictable and also, in a way, richer. From then on I could build "on a solid foundation": I find nothing better than this cliché to express the feeling that overwhelmed me, as ambiguous as it was comforting.

In any case, September came, and then October, November ... *Artforum* didn't come. I should write a story about what it was like to wait for it those many months, but it is impossible because the wait was made up of so many very tiny spiritual movements, so varied, that the story would never end. The fact is, I didn't stop waiting for a single instant of that period of my life. When a new month began, my wait resumed, beginning again from zero as if I had never suffered any disappointment. It would maintain that pristine condition during the entire first week, and then some; then it would start to change color, but, curiously, not strength. The second week fell into the category of an understandable delay due to the mechanics of the postal service; the third week, the same but with nuances of an accident; and finally my wait became contaminated with the tone that prevailed in the fourth week, which was of the inexplicable, of the bureaucratic whims of an institution as large and complex as the international postal service, where "anything can happen." A new month would start, and everything that came before would be erased, the illusion of imminence was reborn, fresh and whole, pure, and the cycle repeated itself. The wait grew tenser at the two extremes; on one hand, they told me that they send the issue to their subscribers before it goes on sale, as soon as it arrives from the printers, maybe a whole week before it is distributed to bookstores and kiosks. I would therefore seriously expect to receive it on day one of each month. But on day ten or fifteen, I could also seriously expect it, because it's a long trip from New York to Buenos Aires, and there can be many obstacles along the way … As for the previous months' issues, those I had not received and had no rational reason to expect, I wouldn't totally give up on them when the next one came out; for them I'd retain a special compartment of hope, a rather murky one because I never developed it consciously. It could be, for example, that they were piling up at the Central Post Office waiting for someone to come and claim them, which I would do as soon as they brought me the corresponding notification, and this was not subject to any calendar date because it depended on them doing an inventory of unclaimed packages, or clearing out their storage room …

Apart from these thoughts, and independently of them, I had another more concrete one regarding the reason I had not received by beloved *Art-*

forum. They stole it at the post office. There was a long tradition of such thefts. Everybody knew that they stole magazines at the post office and then sold them. Knowing this, or suspecting it based on strong evidence, solved nothing. It was sad, but there was nothing to be done. I received very heart-felt condolences from my friends, who told me their own similar stories, the most depressing of which was from a friend who found the used book stall (in Plaza Italia) where the traitorous postal employee sold his magazines, and my friend went there every month to buy it back: he paid twice, but at least he got it. I remembered the many times I had bought *Artforum* at those stalls and my joy at finding them. Suddenly that search itself disheartened me. It seemed impossible, like one of those coincidences that happen in stories, though not in reality. Some-one recommended a practical, though not infallible, solution: rent a post office box in the Central Post Office, thereby eliminating part of the chain (not all of it) where the theft could occur. I rejected this. I would never even consider doing something of the sort. Moreover, this might not be a matter of theft. I have never liked to distrust other people, not only out of my hatred of prejudice but because it seems to me that trust simplifies life and contributes to inner peace. Moreover, the indestructible feelings I have for my postman had spread to all the employees of the Post Office, for he is a kind and guileless man, and one time he asked me why I received so much mail from so many countries. So, every time he rang my bell or stopped me in the street to give me an envelope (because I walk around the neighborhood almost as much as he does), my heart would beat wildly, and I would believe that the moment had arrived ... And because it didn't arrive, that moment was all moments. I continued to receive all kinds of correspondence, and it occurred to me that there was a genius trickster who was transforming the envelope I wanted to receive into another one that contained a bill or an advertisement for a pizzeria.

As far as taking serious and concrete measures, I took none. As has happened to me so many times in my life, I adapted to a situation anybody else would have actively rebelled against. Fatalism? Cowardice? I experienced a strange—twisted, if you wish—kind of satisfaction. I had done everything I could do. Subscribing had been an act so foreign to my normal behavior, so heroic (for me), that I justified my perfect inaction. It was as if, after so much uncertainty, so many mishaps, I had arrived at the end of the road. Nothing more could be demanded of me.

Needless to say, there was (that is: there was not) *Artforum*, my favorite magazine, that unexpected and decontextualized luxury of my provincialism, that inexhaustible source of artistic dream states. I didn't have it, and I didn't stop wanting it. I wanted it more than ever. The situation had something contradictory about it, and even unsustainable. Something had to happen.

But nothing happened. Unless I count a curious fantasy that had overtaken me at the time, more a hallucination than a fantasy, with the insurmountable strength of reality.

I live on the corner of Bonorino and Bonifacio streets. On Bonorino, a few meters away (there are two houses in between), there is a police station, Station #38. The policemen park their patrol cars on the street, near the corner and around it. They are constantly coming and going outside the door to my building, getting in and out of their cars. I noticed that when they were carrying long guns, they would always look to see if they were loaded, check the safety or some other mechanism before they got into their patrol cars. It was almost inevitable to think that sooner or later there would be an accident, that there might be a tiny miscalculation in the movement of their hands, or a flaw in the firearm, and a shot would escape. Above all because around this time the television was full of stories about people being shot by the police because they were caught in the middle of a shoot-out or hit by a stray bullet, or some other similar reason. Certain news items inexplicably become fashionable, and that was the fashion of the moment. An accident might not happen in one hundred years, or it could happen today ... Watching a policeman hold a rifle, it had to occur to me that it would suddenly go off, and hit me. Joining that fleeting fantasy to the fantasy that dominated my life must have been as easy as adding two plus two. The electric buzzer rang while we were having lunch. I answered, because at that hour of the day, which was the hour of the postman, I'd always rush to answer. "Who is it?" "The postman." "I'm coming down." And down I went, skipping four stairs at a time, seized by a delicious expectation streaked with fatalistic caution. I opened the door. The postman's round face appeared, holding a certified letter out to me, and while I was signing he took other envelopes out of his leather satchel ... "This is also for you ..." And there was something more ... I'd already seen it: a white envelope, square, with a logo printed in blue: ARTFORUM. My joy was enormous, the reward after such a long wait, so much disappointment. I took it as if in a dream. Like everything you've waited for for a long time, when it becomes real it loses a large part of its reality, shedding reality in strips along the torturous path of desire. And at the very moment I had it in my hands, a policeman's rifle fired by mistake from across the street, and of all the places where the bullet could have ended up (it had to end up somewhere), it ended in me, in my heart. In front of me was the postman, corpulent and heavy, but the bullet came from the side, diagonally, and it hit me without glancing off him; at first he didn't realize what was happening; the noise was no big deal: a sharp bang that was difficult to locate, like all brief sounds. He saw my body twitch, and perhaps he saw my stunned expression, but he didn't connect cause with effect, he didn't know there was a sequence of cause and effect. I didn't know, either, and I didn't have time to figure it out before I fell, because I was already dying. A large caliber bullet that makes a hole in the delicate compartments of the heart has no mercy. But even so, I had time: I had the supreme instant of death. I doubled over, fell, and the postman, in his shock, didn't manage to catch me; I fell headfirst down the stairs, the envelopes fell out of my hands, all except one, the one that contained the *Artforum*, the happiness of whose possession still endured, anachronistically, mixed in with the sadness of dying, of leaving the world that I loved so much. Who said that a wound in the heart doesn't bleed? My body had turned into a fountain; liters and liters of red blood, which shone like an enormous ruby under the midday sun, formed in a circle around me, a vortex into which I was sinking, forevermore, still clinging to my *Artforum*.

NOVEMBER 12, 2002

Twenty-four Issues of *Artforum*

ON SATURDAY ERNESTO TOLD ME THAT A used bookstore on Avenida de Mayo was selling off part of Ruth Benzacar's library: catalogues, art books, magazines; above all, magazines.

"A lot of them are old issues of *Artforum* ..."

"Really?" I looked at my watch. It was five in the afternoon. "Can we go now?"

He thought for a moment. He knows the hours of all the bookstores in Buenos Aires.

"No, it's closed. It's open Monday through Friday."

"I'll go on Monday."

"Good. Don't wait. I don't think they'll last long."

"When did you see them?"

"On Thursday."

I felt a twinge of irritation. If he had called me immediately, I could have gone on Thursday, or Friday. Now we'd lost two days, and who knows if everything had been laid to waste. But I didn't utter a word of reproach. I don't want to be unfair to Ernesto, to whom I owe so many of my joys as a reader. There had to be an explanation for his lack of urgency, for example, that he didn't think buyers would rush in, or maybe that he didn't fully appreciate the extent of my fanaticism. I didn't give it another thought, out of disgust for that kind of paranoid psychologizing of behavior, but now that I'm writing this I have to admit that these are not satisfactory explanations. Ernesto knows very well, better than anybody, that you can't count on a rare find, no matter how rare it is, staying on the shelves of a bookstore for a day, or even an hour. Just a few weeks earlier we had had this confirmed. He had seen a complete edition (eleven volumes) of Pepys's diary, he told me, we went together the next day, and it had been sold! How many readers are there in Buenos Aires who are interested in that monumental work? And of those, how many have the money to buy it, on the spur of the moment, during our period of crisis? And of those, how many would find out that it had shown up in a little known bookstore on Calle Sarmiento? Nevertheless, there was the result: it was gone. Considering the fact that *Artforum* has more of an audience than Pepys's diaries, and that those issues would be

sold at a derisory price, and that they were at a much
more visible and popular bookstore, there was very
good cause for alarm.

As for the other argument, i.e. that he hadn't
taken the full measure of my interest in *Artforum*,
this was a good reason for perplexed outrage. Did
he not know me at all? He was my confidant, the
only person I hid nothing from! Or at least that's
what I thought. Because one thing is the sincere
intention to tell someone everything, and another
the efficacy with which one makes oneself understood. In that respect it could have been my fault.
An excess of gentility might have led me to give the
impression that my interest in this or that, and in
Artforum, stood merely on the threshold of passion,
as if passion were something vulgar, far below the
likes of us. Had I deceived him so effectively? Or,
better said, had he allowed himself to be so thor-
oughly deceived? Because I'd learned that kind of
gentility from him, and I made him my confidant
because I knew that his dandyism would prevent
him from taking me too seriously ... In any case, I
think the blame was shared, mirrored.

Once we established that there was nothing to
do for now, and that I would go to Avenida de Mayo

on Monday, I asked him, more relaxed now, how
he had found out that the library had belonged to
Ruth Benzacar. From a few dedications, he said.
A renowned gallery owner (we both knew her,
though superficially), Ruth had died, still young, a
few months before. She must have left a good art library, which would remain in the hands of her heirs.
For some reason, probably due to lack of space, they
got rid of magazines and catalogues. The issues of
Artforum were from the eighties.

I made a firm decision to go on Monday morning. But on Sunday Juan Pablo called, and we made
a date to meet at Café Tortoni on Monday at four in
the afternoon, and since this bookstore was a mere
hundred meters from Tortoni (and about half an
hour from my house), it wasn't worth it to make
two trips ... Or was it? I reasoned in the following
way. In the morning and early afternoon some, or
many, of the issues of *Artforum* could be sold. But
I wouldn't know about them. I would be satisfied
with the ones I found, and I wouldn't have anything to blame myself for because the others might
have been sold on Friday. Whatever the case, I lived
those two days in a state of delicious anticipation.

On Monday at three in the afternoon I entered the

bookstore. I went directly to the *Artforum*s, which were on a cart closer to the door. There were a lot: half a meter of magazines stacked vertically, which I began to look at one by one. "I have this, I don't have this, I have this, I don't have this ..." I recognized the issues I had with one glance at the cover. I didn't care about the dates. For me, *Artforum* is always new. I lost count of the issues I didn't have. Decades of searching for them with great effort when there were none, of being happy with only one whenever luck put it within reach, had poorly prepared me for this abundance. So poorly that at a certain point I thought I'd buy two, or three, or at the most four. But how to choose which ones? From the content, obviously. But for that, I was even more poorly prepared. I had always bought *Artforum* by just looking at the cover and making sure I didn't have it at home; it had never occurred to me to look inside to see if it contained material that more or less interested me. What kind of material might that be? I could almost say—and I would if I weren't afraid of being misunderstood—that I didn't care a bit about the content.

Fortunately, I reacted in time. Something inside me said, "I don't want to have regrets for the rest of my life." I would take them all. For once, I would do something crazy, I would get away with it, I would indulge myself ... But what was so crazy about it? The price wasn't a problem: they were very cheap. The space they would take in my house wasn't, either (we had just rented another apartment upstairs from the one we occupied, for books). The time it would take me to read them was even less of a problem, because I had no intention of sitting down and reading them systematically. What, then? Why did that sensation of "crazy" persist?

Probably because there was something demented about buying so many magazines at the same time. Magazines appear periodically and are bought one by one. In some haphazard and fortuitous and anachronistic way, I had been doing this with *Artforum* over a period of many years and decades. You can buy two magazines together (or three, or even four) if you've missed a previous issue for some reason. But who buys many issues together, let's say ten or more, of the same magazine? A collector. And I am not a collector, not at all. Also, a scholar or an archivist might do it, someone dedicated to recuperating the "lost time" of contemporary art. This was a little more like me, but the margin of irony was too wide for me to really be able to identify.

Leaving aside such subtleties, or digging deeper into them, the craziness of buying all of them resided in the excess of pleasure, or at least, gratification. I had had a stroke of luck, there they were in my avid hands, as incredible as they were undeniable, material, tangible. We always count on having strokes of luck, but on a different and fluctuating plane in time, not in the present. Now it was the present. The present and *Artforum* that expressed it now coincided. That was enough to make me slightly giddy with incredulity.

There was also something crazy about the imprudence. Isn't it dangerous to be too happy? Wouldn't it have to be paid back afterwards? Wouldn't it be a better idea to save something for later? The answer is: No.

I simply separated out the ones I didn't have and took them to the counter in the back, in two trips. The salesperson started to count them—I hadn't—and I told her that in the meantime I was going to see if there was anything else that interested me. This made sense. The truth was I didn't want anything else (what more could I want?), but one never knows. Not every day does the library of a renowned gallery owner appear in a used bookstore—even though it was the extra and rejected part of the library, it could offer opportunities that would never come again. For my part, it was more than anything a gesture of normality: I was not, and did not want to be, a compulsive or blind buyer of my favorite magazine, but rather an educated reader with a wide range of tastes, one who believes, rightly so, that art doesn't begin and end with *Artforum*. And there was something else, something more fundamental: *Artforum* was not an end in itself. I will not fully develop this idea because it would lead me too far astray. In the end, of course, it was the art. *Artforum* was the first step along the road that led to that end, the eternal, immense, and marvelous first step. Afterwards came all the other steps, one of which, very close to the first (I would say it was the second), was paved with the books by critics who wrote for *Artforum*, or those about artists who appeared in *Artforum* . . .

That's why I went back to the tables. But I was in too much of a rush to leave with my treasure to carry out a systematic search. I didn't see anything. My normality didn't stretch that far.

Nevertheless, I did add something. Nothing very well thought out. An impulse buy, something simply beautiful, attractive, strange, that anybody in my place would have bought. But afterwards, when I thought about it, I noticed that my choice had some significant features. It was a small orange book, hardcover, exquisitely printed on glossy paper, full-color reproductions on every recto page and text on every verso page, the catalogue of an exhibit of miniature art (*At the Threshold of the Visible, Minuscule and Small-Scale Art*, 1964–1996 Independent Curators Incorporated, New York, 1997).

Moreover, I didn't have much time: time had also shrunk: when I looked at my watch it was already four o'clock, so I paid and left, carrying two large bags. Juan Pablo was waiting for me in Tortoni. I showed him my finds. He had been friends with Ruth Benzacar and had worked for years in her gallery. He told me that Ruth's apartment on Calle Talcahuano had just been sold, which explained the liquidation of part of her library. Then followed a few melancholic reflections on the void left by that energetic promoter of Argentinean art, on the brevity of life, and on how unpredictable destiny was, after which we moved on to another subject.

Juan Pablo is one of those men who is very attentive to the preferences and obsessions of others, perhaps because he is always willing to incorporate them into his own repertoire. Years before, when we first met, he found out about my weakness for *Artforum*, and he also began looking for it and buying it, and since then every time he saw one in some bookstore or museum shop or in one of those magazine brothels on Calle Corrientes, he would call or write to let me know. He did the same thing when he found out about my passion for pens. Here I must say that pens are the only other passion that can compete in my soul with what I feel for *Artforum*. I never have enough of one or of the other.

The purpose of this meeting in Tortoni was ostensibly to offer a toast and take stock of the work we had done throughout the year, and to say goodbye for the rest of the summer, because he was going to Córdoba for vacation. One detail that shows his mimetic nature: when the waiter came, I hesitated for a moment and then ordered a whisky. Although it was early, the euphoria I felt from the purchase of the magazines and the feeling that I could not expect anything more from the day made me think that the occasion deserved something special. He ordered the same, and when I told him that he should not feel obliged to accompany me, he said that he had, in fact, also felt like having a whisky and had been afraid I would order a coffee, in which case he would not have dared to order alcohol. Because he expresses himself with a bit of exaggeration and bombast, he painted this fear as an anguished panic, and the good fortune that my wishes had coincided with his own was a relief befitting a condemned men who received a reprieve at the very last moment. We toasted.

Knowing him, I should have anticipated that the toast was merely an excuse for something else. In fact, I didn't have to wait long for the surprise. It was a gift. He had no reason to give it to me, except for that pleasure, which I know so well, of leaving a material trace of moments of friendship. Something tangible, independent of memory. It was a pen. I lifted it over my head. Some day I will create a catalogue *raisonné* of my pens.

This one was rare and beautiful. A perfectly cylindrical tube made of gold and porcelain. The very short cap and the base were made of gold, as well as the nib. The rest was black, white, and gold porcelain in wavy veins. Total simplicity, except for two tiny round buttons of opaque black coral, one on the cap and one on the barrel, and Juan Pablo told me that he hadn't figured out what their function was. I couldn't see any either, and assumed they were decorations. Later I understood: they were to prevent the pen, covered or uncovered, from rolling and falling off the edge of the table onto the ground. They were really useful because I've had this kind of accident more than once.

The porcelain and the unusual shape seemed to defy true elegance, whose essential requirement is simplicity and not calling attention to itself. But in this case they were justified because they turned an object that otherwise would have been only ostentatious and expensive into a curiosity. The eccentricity compensated for the expense, and in Juan Pablo's language of good manners, it meant something like: "I saw it as so strange that I couldn't resist the temptation to bring it to you."

The day ended with a few other small gratifications, not the least of which was showing my trophies to my family. It was December 6, 2002, one of those days that makes you think that if all of life were like that it would be perfect. Twenty-four issues of *Artforum* (because there were twenty-four, I counted them when I got home), a difficult record to match, and on top of that, a beautiful pen. One can say that they are only material objects, that other things bring true happiness. But would that be true? There always has to be something material, even love needs something to touch. And in my proceeds of that joyful day, the material was so entwined with the spiritual that it transcended itself, without ceasing to be material. I won't talk about the pen, I would get too carried away. But that transcendence was pretty obvious in the magazines. They were paper and ink, and they were also ideas and reveries. They reproduced the dialectic of art, with as many or more attributes as art itself. Before, I spoke about the "material trace." It was more than that: the word is "luxury." Material made of spirit is the luxurious border where reality communicates with utopia.

JANUARY 27, 2003

The Clothespins

WITHIN THE DAILY ROUTINE OF THE HOUSE-
hold, small inexplicable incidents also occur. Why
did it happen, why didn't it happen? Nobody knows.

All we know is that something happened. What?
Well ... so many things! Something is always happening, and it's difficult to set one incident, one an-
ecdote, apart. How to know what deserves mention?
One should talk all the time, or remain silent forever.
The trifles that feed innocent chatter sink into the
subsoil of the silence of the responses. Sometimes a
chance repetition insinuates a meaning.

"Another clothespin broke! What bad luck!"

"I'll fix it." (I thought that the spring that con-
nects the two halves had gotten detached.)

"No. It broke. It can't be fixed."

"Throw it away!"

"Throw it away!"

The laundry room is to the left of my study, which
was originally the servants' quarters. Presiding over

47

the ceiling of the laundry room is the clothesline, a rack of parallel wires with a tubular metal frame. It is set up and taken down with a complicated system of pulleys. That's where we hang the clothes to dry— usually the northern light filters through a jungle of damp garments before it reaches my chair in front of the computer. On the rare occasions when there are no clothes hanging, I like to look at the empty parallel lines above me, the idle many-colored clothespins sitting like little birds on the wires.

"Another clothespin broke!"

The feeling of repetition. Hadn't it already broken? No, this is another one! That makes three. That makes four! We've got to talk about this.

Suddenly, in the silence of inspiration … Snap! I look, and a clothespin is lying on the floor, broken, and at the same time a wet shirt drops a sleeve, then shakes it for an instant as it drips, as if pointing to itself as it falls. An insignificant accident: not sufficient to modify my taciturn habits. Nonetheless, it registers, and returns later when the washing machine is opened, and comments and complaints can be heard while the clothes are being hung up.

"Another one! What are they making them out of? Oh, no, one more!"

"Huh? What? What's going on?"

"These clothespins, in the last few days I can't count how many have broken … It's unbelievable. Ten years go by, and the same clothespins are still working, I forget … What am I saying ten years! Twenty, thirty. I have clothespins from before we got married. And now they're all breaking at the same time."

"Hmm … Now that I remember … Today I was writing and suddenly, snap! One broke, and plink! plank! The pieces fell on the floor."

"Did it break on its own?"

"On its own."

"You didn't walk underneath and your head got caught on the clothes and … ?"

"On its own, on its own! I was just sitting here."

"How weird. But it's true, I picked up the pieces and threw them in the garbage."

"No, I picked up the pieces, and I threw them out."

"Maybe it was another one? What color was it?"

"Blue."

"Didn't I tell you! The one I picked up was yellow."

And after several, how weird! how really weird! how crazy is that! the subject was filed away. Until another clothespin falls, and another, and another.

"Maybe you're handling them too roughly? I had an aunt, and they wouldn't let her wash the dishes because she always broke them, her hands were too strong."

"Come on, please! Never . . . ! Always . . . !"

Anyway, they break on their own. We have to accept the evidence. Nobody breaks them. They break all on their own. Soon there is a veritable downpour, we have to sweep up the pieces with a broom. The ominous crack, the fall, the clatter on the floor of the laundry room.

"There's nothing we can do. I'm going to have to go buy clothespins. I'd almost forgotten that clothespins can be bought."

"I'll go!"

"We have to buy at least a dozen."

"Or two."

"Or two. At this rate, soon we won't have any left."

"I'm going to buy a gross. Do you know what a gross is? It's a dozen dozen."

"You and your exaggerations."

The pieces need to be picked up and carefully examined. Broken, split. They are small, fragile objects, but not that fragile. And almost nothing is so fragile that it breaks on its own. Poorly made, surely, poorly assembled, poorly cut, with defects. One could blame the lack of quality control in Argentinean industry: unless these were imported, from Taiwan, from Brazil. Who knows. However ... they're from different batches, some are ancient, rotten, almost shapeless, dented. They must not be that bad if they've lasted decades. So, what?

The truth is, their time had come. Poor things.

There's something called "material fatigue," and this could be what's happening to the clothespins. But this argument doesn't stand up to scrutiny. It's not only that the clothespins that are expiring are of different ages, but they're also made of different materials: some are plastic, others are wood, still others are metal. The only thing they have in common is that they are clothespins, have the form of clothespins. In any case we would need to talk about "form fatigue."

I can more or less understand material fatigue, or imagine it: the atoms get looser and looser, their electrons run out of batteries, some die and leave holes where the orbits of others get twisted, the empty spaces start filling up with dust, the mass weakens with age ... But forms? The material fatigue that holds them up could affect them, that's true. But that wasn't the case here, I could prove it by touch, because the wood, the plastic, and the metal of the pieces of the dead clothespins was solid, without any sign of disintegration. So there was no choice but to surrender to the evidence: there existed such a thing as form fatigue, still not diagnosed by science, and I had witnessed its first manifestation.

It seems that there were no antecedents. Forms had always enjoyed good health, and endurance against all odds, as shown by the extravagant acrobatics artists forced them to perform. What hadn't they done to them, and they'd always emerged victorious and unscathed. But nothing was eternal. Their immaterial and abstract condition had preserved them till now from the natural wearing away of things, but maybe their hour had come. If it was really a process of extinction, how would it unfold? Maybe it would be slow, millenary, fatigue didn't necessarily mean extinction, perhaps some forms would die before others, and the clothespins were the forerunners (thinking about the contortions artists had subjected them to, I remembered the enormous clothespin of Claes Oldenburg). We could allow time for man's ingenuity, or the implacable advancement of science, to find a solution, though it would not be as easy to solve as material fatigue; what to do, for example, with the remnants of forms? And in the worst-case scenario, we would be left in a world without forms — maybe it was better this way. Maybe we have lived as prisoners of something that in reality we don't need.

Conjectures

AFTER MY SUBSCRIPTION WAS SORTED OUT, my problems weren't over: new ones were created. Because such things are never fully sorted. The first two weeks of each month was the approximate span of time when one could reasonably expect the magazine to arrive. But it was more reasonable to wait a few days more. The truly reasonable thing would have been not to wait at all, but this was completely beyond my capabilities. I waited with fury, day after day, and within each day, hour after hour. I will not dwell on the vast number of suspenseful anecdotes, though they are all seared into my memory. Nor on the infinite conjectures I indulged in. I will tell only two.

One was the cleaning of the building where we live. It's a small building, and we don't have a doorman. A young couple comes to wash the sidewalk and the stairwell three times a week; on rare occasions both of them, usually they take turns, and they come very early in the morning, so early that we almost never see them; we deduce they've been here because the sidewalk is wet or the floors of the foyer and landings are shiny from recent waxing. I'm the one to check for these signs because I'm the first to get up and go out. In any case, two or three times in a row it so happened that the day they came to clean, *Artforum* arrived. That was enough for me to establish (that is: invent) an ad hoc causality: they had to come to clean in order for the postman to bring me joy. Just like that, without explanations, for no reason. It's strange that I didn't seek, while I was at it, a magical reason, for example, this one that occurs to me now: that the building had to be pristine in order for the *Artforum* to deign to disembark therein. Even without these ornate embroideries, it didn't take long for a small allusive folklore to be created in my family. My wife reproached me for mocking the supernatural, an element she fervently believes in. She warned me that I shouldn't play with fire. I responded that I wasn't playing, that I was taking it very seriously. She didn't believe me. I closed my ears to the criticism, and I led by example. The kids, when they returned at dawn from their night out and found the cleaners, would leave me a note in the kitchen to let me know. And whenever the coincidence occurred, we would look at each other while moving our heads in a vertical line: we had to give ourselves over to the evidence, believe it or not. Parenthetically I will say that I subjected my entire family to a vicarious and fairly impatient form of suspense; when the magazine did finally arrive, they'd breath a sigh of relief at no longer having to tolerate, at least for a few weeks, my monomaniacal anxiety. And once it arrived, and the issue for the following month had not yet come out, I would manifest my astonishment every time the couple came to clean. "Why do they come, *Artforum* already arrived? Maybe for reasons of hygiene?"

The other conjecture (the other I want to recount, there were many others) had to do with bread. There's a bakery right in front of the house, and since it's so close and we have only to cross the street, we've gotten used to waiting to buy bread till the very last moment. This means: when lunch is ready and my wife calls us to set the table. We used to send our eldest son, but because of this issue with the postman, I never miss an opportunity to go downstairs and take an extra look at the mailbox. So I go. And often a special situation unfolds.

We always buy the same amount of bread, an amount that costs seventy centavos. Knowing what a drama it is for a retail merchant to give change, I try to pay with the right amount. Of course for daily customers like us, the baker is not going to refuse to give us change even if we pay him with large bills; he could always charge us the following day. But I make an effort to bring the right amount. As I said, the trip across the street to the bakery happens at the last moment, sometimes with a touch of urgency, sometimes we are already sitting down to eat, and I, lost in my reading, have lost track of time and run out (because I can't eat without fresh bread on the table). But no matter how much of a rush I'm in, I take the time to put my hands in my pockets to make sure I have the correct coins. And it might be that I find a single one peso coin . . . Here I need to explain that in Buenos Aires coins have extra value: without them you can't ride the bus because the blasted little ticket machines accept only coins. In my family we are assiduous patrons of public transportation, which is one reason we particularly appreciate coins, and we consider it a waste to use them for a purchase. So when they see my coin, unique and precious, they rush to offer me two-peso bills, because by paying with one of them we not only save a peso coin but we also obtain one peso thirty centavos more in change. But I refuse! They keep protesting and I'm already skipping down the stairs ... Because the idea has just occurred to me that by spending that coin, that last coin, I am making a sacrifice to fate in order to enable the arrival of my beloved magazine.

The conclusion I hoped to reach with this story of some of my tocades, was the following: the most dissimilar facts can be connected in such a way that they participate in the same story, and their incoherence can become coherent. If you get a call for the wrong number, it's going to rain. If a pigeon alights on the balcony rail, there's going to be a subway strike. If a country changes its name, a relative is going to die. There are no restrictions, there are no forbidden subjects, the entire universe in its innumerable manifestations is at our disposal. The only restriction is chance, which doesn't restrict anything because it is by definition what allows for everything and places in communication the beings that are most remote as well as those that are closest to each other, crossing over levels, planes, languages.

Nobody believes in what's unbelievable, but we

all surrender to superstitions in one way or another.
Superstition is the plausible part of the supernatural. It is sustained by desire, enthusiasm, necessity,
which flesh it out, anchoring it in life and justifying
all the shapes it takes.

A solid and coherent system of superstitions is a
religion, and an entire civilization can be built from
there. But before and after that system comes the invention of superstition, the creative act, whose de-
sirous economy incorporates all the datum of the
imagination.

That's how superstition turns the most capricious
and unexpected configurations of reality into signs.
The way we read those signs is riddled with great
perplexity. How did they come into the world, how
did they come together, how did they come to have
meaning? What unknown stories are behind them?

I remember in the sixties and seventies, when hal-
lucinogens were in fashion, artisanal drugs would
appear whose efficacy posed a similar problem.
The question arose: how were they discovered? It
didn't seem like those hippies were following the
scientific method. Might they have used "trial and
error"? For example, they smoked sun-dried to-
mato seeds mixed with corn silk and had beautiful,

colorful visions. But where did they get the recipe? Had they first tried with flax, apple, or watermelon seeds, rejecting each in turn when they didn't produce any effect? With cardoon strands, baby hairs, fermented mustard? Impossible. There were too many elements to test and mix, all of nature, magnetized by the desire to "expand consciousness" beyond Reason.

DECEMBER 20, 2003

A New Calendar

TODAY, DECEMBER 6, I INVENTED A NEW WAY
of numbering the days, and the result is: today is
November 42. This might seem absurd, but it is
very well-reasoned, based on my wait for *Artforum*.
I'll explain how I came up with it. Suppose a new
month arrives, *Artforum* comes out over there, in
New York, it is to be assumed that it's on its way,
I'm already waiting for it. Suppose on the twentieth,
it hasn't yet arrived: I've spent twenty days waiting
for it. Suppose it doesn't arrive on the twenty-fifth,
the thirtieth ... The month ends. It's the fifth of the
following month: I've spent thirty-five days waiting! Or rather, for me, today is the thirty-fifth! The
thirty-fifth! Who says a month can't have thirty-five
days? But, just a moment ... If it's the fifth, I've also
spent five days waiting for this month's *Artforum*,
which also of course hasn't arrived ... And the two
waits, or "the waits for the two of them," overlap and

are added together. Or rather, today is not only the thirty-fifth, it's the fortieth!

That's why I say that today is November 42: the thirty days of November plus the six of December, make thirty-six. Plus, again, those same six days of December, which make up the wait for the December *Artforum*: forty-two. Today is November 42. Months get longer, they can even become years, and they overlap with other months that are also very long, made up of double or triple days.

This subject inspires me, fills my head with numbers. For example, let's say three months go by and I don't receive anything—for instance, the months of November, December, and January (we have to take into account which months because some have thirty and some have thirty-one days). Thirty in November plus thirty-one in December plus thirty-one in January, that makes ninety-two, which corresponds to my wait for November's *Artforum*, plus sixty-two for my wait for December's, plus thirty-one for January's: one hundred eighty-five. Or rather, the last day of January would be November 185. If I said to someone who doesn't know my habits and thoughts, "today is November 185," they'd think I was crazy (they'd have other reasons, besides).

Melancholy

ARTFORUM HASN'T ARRIVED. A STATE OF deep melancholy has taken hold of me. I see the world through a gray veil, not even the best of jokes can exact a smile from me. I could die right now and I wouldn't notice the difference. Or maybe I would.

It might seem like nothing. After all, nothing horrible has happened to me; but I don't need to compare my problem with those of so many people who have really serious ones. There is, however, always a lack of proportion when it comes to the human soul. Moreover, melancholy as an effect is neither great nor small, important nor insignificant, serious nor frivolous; it's more like nothingness. It's not so much that it doesn't have any attributes as that it dilutes all of them in an impenetrable fog.

And if I fantasize about the arrival of what I'm waiting for, about the satisfaction of my desire ... the sadness still persists: in my fantasy I see myself

halfheartedly leafing through an *Artforum*, or holding it on my lap without even opening it, staring off
into space, expressionless, bitter. I wouldn't have
expected something like this from my optimistic
character, from my ability to find contentment in
small things, in minimums, including minimums
of meaning. I never would have imagined myself in
that position, because I had always taken for granted
that it was the world that was depressed and that I
was creating diversions, pulling them out of my fes-
tive soul. But so it is, and I feel as if this melancholy
were irreversible. It's as if it had waited for centuries
and millennia to ripen, as if it came from the depths
of an antiquity that I didn't know I had inside me,
and once it has opened its black corolla it will never
be able to close it again. It's an eternity, which waiting merely placed into time.

DECEMBER 14, 2003

My Very Own Artforum

EVENTUALLY (BUT THIS HAPPENED YEARS ago: I am trying to recover a memory that I've half lost along the bumpy trajectory of my life) I began to get tired of waiting, tired of the psychic space waiting put me in. I wanted to adopt a more virile stance. Living in a state of expectation was eroding my nerves, distracting me from my occupations or directly nullifying them. Nothing was left. Waiting is an empty waste of time.

Wasn't it a little absurd? Wasn't I asking for the impossible? The entire mechanism of chance that had to be set in motion in order for the magazine to reach me, the necessary integrities and efficacies. A miracle. One couldn't ask for a miracle to be repeated and with the punctuality that I hoped for. Experience had showed this to me a thousand times, but I remained obstinate ... I must have derived some pleasure from continuing to insist, perhaps the pleasure of identity. As if *Artforum* were myself.

How many thousands of kilometers did it have to travel, that bundle of colored paper? These days the yakety-yak about globalization tries to persuade us that all places are the same place; that might be, but that place is full of distances, and some of them are enormous. That great and so highly praised contiguity is valid for information, but not for physical objects that transport it. Thinking about this I realized that if I were offered the entire content of *Artforum* without *Artforum*, I wouldn't be interested. Just thinking about it, I felt profound disinterest, almost scorn. Was this, then, fetishism of the object? My vainglorious information about Contemporary Art was merely a masquerade to hide a puerile longing for possession?

But it is common knowledge that when children ask you to buy them something they are also asking for something else, which remains secret, and this is one of those secrets that are never revealed, not even on the psychoanalyst's couch. That's where I might find the key to my infinite wait for *Artforum*. What I was waiting for was something else, which was hiding in the invisible shell of the Other. I could extend the simile, based on how infantile the whole thing is: children ask for toys, which are almost always representations. The entire complex of representation was set into motion by an art magazine. I wasn't surprised, then, when I began to suspect that *Artforum* had entered my life, so many years before, in order to signify something else, which had neither name nor form, and to give me something palpable and periodic around which to implement the movements of my soul in reference to that other arcane thing. Could that be? It was very possible. It would explain such a persistent fixation, so different from my fickle psyche that changes interests every few months or weeks. If I think about it a little, it doesn't make much sense to remain attached to the same magazine for almost my entire adult life, during which thousands of books have passed through my hands, as well as the experience of traveling, the people I've met, the innumerable vicissitudes of my family, professional, and social life.

Turning *Artforum* into a cloaking object clearly had a worrisome side. And a sad side, as well, because it downgraded it to a symbolic gadget, a device, and it made me feel I'd wasted all the time and effort I had devoted to it. The worrisome part was that underneath it there appeared—or better said, there was hiding—a fearful presence, a powerful entity that had adopted it to disguise itself. If it went to so much trouble to not show itself, it must have its reasons, which couldn't not worry me. Underneath an innocent hobby, a picturesque eccentricity, there crouched something nameless (the meaning of a sign that had occupied my thoughts forever), which could just as well be lethal as the key to a new life.

In a fit of enthusiasm (or panic: they are so similar) I decided to take the bull by the horns and abandon the passivity with which I had dealt with the issue till then. It couldn't be that difficult: it was enough to transfer the hyperactivity that had characterized my literary activity into the field of servile and pusillanimous waiting. I could make my own personal *Artforum*, one that depended on my will and obeyed my tempo.

Accustomed as I am to discard my ideas and feel ashamed of them the following day, the objections leaped out at me: I returned to my childhood and remembered the crazy people who painted furniture on the walls of their empty rooms ... But I pushed them aside and immediately began to make plans; I always immediately start planning how to put my ideas into practice because of my embedded terror of forgetting them; on the other hand,

I always find a good excuse to put off carrying out those plans; I can wait eternities, literally eternities, because the moment never arrives.

The first thing I tackled was the size: I would make it square, the same proportions but smaller than the real one, like a scaled reproduction. This was appropriate, moreover, because the size of the magazine always seemed awkward to me. I would reduce it by a quarter, as well as the number of pages; it could be thirty-two pages, one signature, which would allow me to attach the pages to the spine. I would paint the cover, gallery advertisements, illustrations accompanying the articles, all in full color, in water colors (any abstract scribbles would do). I would, of course, write the articles myself. Since I'd be doing this for me alone, I wouldn't need to torture myself with self-criticism or what others will say, which is what happened to me and still happens to me whenever I write essays or articles or talks. I could rave at will, which would go well with the avant-gardism of the subject, better than in the model, which confines itself to serious academic jargon.

The previous paragraph suggests something shoddy, but the intention was quite different. I could make something exquisite, for example, by using particularly fine, antique, Japanese paper. Already the fact of it being unique would, in a way, guarantee its quality, making it more an evaluation of me than of the resulting product. Taking everything into account, in the first place taking into account that I was a patron of the magazine, ethe replica I proposed was a work of art, an original artistic project, which could well have been presented in a flattering article in *Artforum*.

And there was a marginal benefit that immediately attained a towering centrality: time. The time I had lost waiting would be transmuted into time gained: the time of creation. I had by chance hit upon what I had always been looking for: a way to occupy my time that would give me all the satisfaction I could expect from my intellectual interests without placing any conditions on myself that made it difficult. A handicraft for happy people.

My work as a writer was a constant repetition of time's surrender to waiting. I never could, and in fact never wanted to, write for more than one hour, and I spent the vast remainder of each day impatiently waiting for the next one. And within that hour the pattern of the day is repeated: I think of something and together with the thought comes its formulation. In a few seconds it's written, and then I have to wait till I think of something else, something which doesn't happen. I don't want to dig more deeply into this, but I fear that within a few seconds that very thing is going to happen again.

From my earliest childhood I had the problem of empty time, of afternoons as ominous as the gaping mouth of an abyss. The solutions I searched for were always precarious, sometimes deplorable, worse than the problem. For example, doing translations, which became a burden, and didn't even serve their purpose because I would have to quit in the middle of the morning, my head and back aching. Or making excursions to magazine stands downtown to look for issues of *Artforum* that I didn't find, only to return tired, having aggravated my multiple sites of tendinitis, and throw myself into an armchair and stare at the television set with my mind as dried up as a prehistoric grapevine.

This mechanism of the idea and its formulation, which in writing exhausted itself in the moment, could last longer if the idea were for a drawing, and it had to be drawn. It took hours to make a good drawing—detailed, shaded, perhaps with color, as well (and with my ineptness it might require ten tries). Sculpture would have been even better, but I wasn't that delirious. Of course, I had to learn to draw, and without any natural talent for the visual, I would have to resort to I don't know what kind of tricks in order to turn out something presentable. The difficulties discouraged me in advance. I transferred it all to writing, and the stories I wrote were filled with vicarious visuality, as boring for readers as they were ineffectual in occupying my time. That's where *Artforum* entered my life, vicarious to the second degree, a place to hide under double lock and key the secret of nothingness. When I perfected the device by buying a subscription, the time turned (I turned it) into waiting: empty and useless as it continued to be, as a result of it, the waiting ended when it was over. I knowingly confined myself to the vicious circle. How pathetic.

Making my own *Artforum* set this inverted dialectic to rights. I could make one a day, or two if I felt like it, one in the morning and one in the afternoon. I didn't lack inspiration, above all because I didn't need it. In short, I don't know why I didn't do it after so much planning and justification. I'll never forgive myself.

THEN ONE DAY *ARTFORUM* STOPPED COMING altogether. A month passed, then two, then three ... There was no reason for such a thing to happen, my subscription hadn't expired, but the dates came and went, and it didn't arrive. This wasn't an issue of a delay or an accident. A different dimension had opened up, a lack of being, not a lack of mere presence or possession. I realized this change because of the effect it had on me, or better said, the lack of effect. I didn't care. Far from despairing as I had before, I lived with resigned indifference. If I thought about *Artforum*, which happened every once in a while, at long last it was shrouded in the echoes of gentle nostalgia, as can imbue a remote and happy time of life, or the past in general.

But, yes, I did remember it. Not every day, nor every year, but a chance event, a word, an image, would bring it back to mind, not without surprise, as can be provoked by the appearance of a stranger who turns out to be a close relative we had lost sight of. Its invocation had nothing to do with contemporary art, or magazines; on the contrary, in that case the blatancy negated the connection. No. It could be a leaf falling from a tree, the blast of a car horn, some children playing ball in the plaza, the color of the sky at dawn. It came accompanied by a vague sense of futility, which was also futile.

It was as if my youth had been worn out from overuse; I had abused it, as do so many writers who squeeze it until they've extracted every last drop of passion. I confess that I would have preferred the rowdy feeling of catastrophe, but I couldn't find it in myself; I looked for it in my friends, a reflex, and I told them so. They took it quite calmly. The most they said to me was that I was going to stop being "up-to-date." I was perplexed. Is that what they had thought all this time? That I read *Artforum* to keep myself informed about the latest news in the art world? Such a thing had never occurred to me. That would have diminished the magazine, placed it on the level of a vulgar almanac. In any case, and now that they were telling me, I could think that my deepest purpose was to make myself un-up-to-date, or, more precisely, abandon, with an Eastern gesture, the active stance, and let the World, Nature, the Universe, be up-to-date in respect to me. Let Time itself do that.

Nor would I have accepted them telling me that I had read enough on the subject, that nobody could tell me anything new ... If the subject was contemporary art, its nature was that there was always something more to say about it. This is what distinguished it from all other cultural manifestations, which ended up constructing something on the basis of accumulation and organization. Contemporary art had been for me a disappearance, the anachronism that revealed the flight of thought.

In short, it wasn't worth it to look for explanations. I had to live, to continue to live. At this point, I could say: I have reached this point, this that I am is what *Artforum* has made me. And then, finally, I can start to be what I am, without waiting for anything.

ADAM WAS THE WISEST OF MEN, NOBODY will ever emulate his wisdom, clairvoyance, understanding. This is because he was close to the origins, closer than anybody else was able or will ever be able to be. When he came, the world already existed: otherwise he wouldn't have had a place to come to. But it was a world that had only just concluded the preliminary process of appearing, and it had barely begun to accommodate its elements. Adam's marvelous eyes, which learned to see, saw how the atoms—new, brand new—began to trace their orbits, still hesitantly, not knowing exactly how to function. Colors shone one by one, in the gentle fluoride tones that they would never recover when they matured. Space stretched out, dimensions scampered along hallways of burnished ozone, like small children looking for toys. Time had not stopped tightening the spring that it would

later release a little at a time. Adam could almost
touch the edge of the universe, which was expand-
ing like the corolla of a flower preparing to be the
All. Forms were born, wrapped in the shimmering
dampness, they grew sharper as they felt their way
along, successively adopting the line, the plane, vol-
ume, aligning themselves in the perspective of an
infinite trompe l'oeil. Gravity intervened and each
thing making its debut found its place—mountains
and suns, galaxies and roses. Adam heard the very
first birdsong.